Taking Care
of the
EARTH

By Billy Goodman
Illustrated by Kate Gleeson

A GOLDEN BOOK • NEW YORK
Western Publishing Company, Inc., Racine, Wisconsin 53404

© 1992 Western Publishing Company, Inc. Illustrations © 1992 Kate Gleeson. All rights reserved.
Printed in the U.S.A. No part of this book may be reproduced or copied in any form without written
permission from the publisher. All trademarks are the property of Western Publishing Company, Inc.
Library of Congress Catalog Card Number: 91-73426 ISBN: 0-307-11532-1   MCMXCV

Take Care of the Earth

The Earth is a beautiful place. But if people aren't careful, it won't always be. There are many things we can all do to help. If everyone does lots of little things every day, a big thing is going to happen: The Earth will be a cleaner, healthier place.

Here are some things *you* can do to help take care of the Earth....

Take Care of the Earth by Saving Water

Turn off the faucet while you brush your teeth. You'll stop all that water from going right down the drain.

Keep a container of cold drinking water in the refrigerator. Then you won't have to let the tap run until the water gets cold.

Collect rainwater for watering houseplants or a small garden.

Turn off faucets carefully. Lots of drips add up to lots of water lost.

Take showers instead of baths. It may not seem like it, but showers use a lot less water!

Take Care of the Earth by Saving Energy

Turn off electric lights when leaving the room
(and turn off the TV when no one is watching it).

Quickly find what you need in the refrigerator and then close the door. It takes a lot of electricity to keep a refrigerator cold—so try not to let the cold air out!

Walk or ride your bike to nearby places—instead of asking to be driven. This helps save gasoline.

When inside your house on cold days, dress
warmly and block any drafts you notice. Don't
turn up the heat too high!

Remove lint from the clothes dryer. This makes it work more efficiently—which saves energy.

Take Care of the Earth by Recycling

Separate newspapers, bottles, and cans for recycling—instead of dumping them.

Save plastic bags. Wash them and dry them and then use them again!

Save your old drawings. You can always add to
them or draw on the back.

Recycling can really make people happy. Try giving your old toys to someone who can use them (instead of throwing them away) and watch a smile grow.

Take Care of the Earth by Growing Plants

Plant a tree. Give it lots of love and it will keep the air fresh and clean for a long, long time.

Grow houseplants and flowers. Not only are they good for the Earth—plants are beautiful, too!

Give a pretty flowering plant as a gift.

If you take care of the Earth…

the Earth will take care of you.